for Precious Girls Who Are
Kind and Loving

Operation
Kindness

By Cindy Kenney
Illustrated by the Precious Moments Creative Studio

Precious Moments # 918021 (Tradepaper)
          # 918020 (Hardcover)

Library of Congress Control Number: 2008909670

ISBN 978-0-981715 9-2-6 (Tradepaper)
ISBN 978-0-9817159-3-3 (Hardcover)

Printed in China

Table of Contents

CHAPTER ONE

Giggles and Glances

"Hey, everybody," said Avery, as she dunked a tomato in dip. "Why did the tomato blush?"

"Beats me," said Becca, munching popcorn.

"He saw the salad dressing!"

Giggles galore!

I was glowing inside. My living room was filled with new friends, all laughing and chatting. I was beginning to feel that I—Katie Bennett—really *did* belong to this town we had moved to just this year. When Daddy took the job as camp director in Shine, Wisconsin, I didn't think I'd ever fit in. But then Mom and Aunt Ella helped me start a brand-new club—and now look. Lots of friends— lots of laughs—this was super great!

"I've got a joke," Lidia announced, adjusting her overalls. "On the first day of kindergarten, a teacher told her class, 'If you have to go to the bathroom, just raise your hand.' One little boy at the back of her class said, 'How is *that* going to help?' "

Hoots and hollers! Even my puppy Patches yapped at that one. He's an honorary member of the Precious Girls Club. That's the club I started (with help from my family—and it did take a little bit of faith). We meet every Friday after school to have fun and plan ways to share our gifts and talents. And right now, that talent was . . . cracking each other up!

"My turn," I called. "A guy goes to the doctor and says, 'Doctor, please help me! Some days I wake up feeling like Mickey Mouse and other days I wake up feeling like Donald Duck.' The doctor looks at the man and says, 'So, tell me— how long have you been having these Disney spells?' "

Fits of laughter. My joke was a hit! Wow— that made me feel good. My new friends liked me.

"I told a joke yesterday at lunch," began Kirina. We were all waiting for the joke, but Kirina just frowned. "Jenny ruined it by telling everybody the punch line before I had a chance," she finished.

Ooo . . . what a downer. Jenny McBride is a member of our club.

"How come she's so late today?" I asked.

"She probably wants to make a grand entrance," Nicola said.

"You think so?" Becca asked. "Well . . . sometimes she does act like she's a queen."

"My daddy will do anything I ask him to do!" I said, mimicking Jenny perfectly.

Everybody laughed. Hey, I was pretty good at this funny stuff. But why didn't I *feel* as good that time?

"Sometimes she can be kinda mean," Kirina added. "She really hurt Bailey's feelings the other day."

"It's okay," Bailey said quietly, blushing.

"No, it's not!" Nicola protested. Nicola is older than the rest of us. She doesn't put up with Jenny's attitude.

"Jenny *can* be lots of fun," said Avery.

"Sure, but let's face it—when she gets into a mood, she thinks she can treat people any way she wants to," Nicola added.

"Yeah, and I get tired of it," Lidia pouted.

"Hellooooo, my dears," Aunt Ella breezed into the room with her arms full of bags and craft materials. We exchanged quick glances. How much had she heard of our "Jenny" conversation?

Aunt Ella set the bags and materials down and handed out felt, scissors, and supplies.

"We've got a great deal to do to finish the puppets in time for the Shine Festival," she said cheerily. "The children at the hospital will be so delighted to be included in the day's festivities."

"But we haven't even convinced Mr. Boxer to *let* us do the show yet," Becca reminded her.

Aunt Ella gave us a twinkly smile. "I have a feeling that you precious girls will find a way to convince him. After all—he's *just* a busy hospital president. No big deal, right?"—and she grinned at me.

Whew! I thought. *I guess Aunt Ella hadn't heard us talking about Jenny.* Good thing too. After all, here we were meeting to do works of kindness, making puppets to put on a puppet show for the sick kids at Shine Community Hospital. It wouldn't be good to be caught gossiping about a friend—even if Jenny *did* deserve it sometimes.

Just then, I felt a light breeze and saw a swirl of sparkling pastel colors in the air. "Oh, Jenny *deserves* it, huh?" said a tiny voice in my ear.

Now, you may think this was my conscience talking. In a way, you'd be right. But the fact is, it was Faith—my guardian angel. Having my very own guardian angel—who no one can see or hear but me—is pretty cool, *most* of the time. But not when she reads my thoughts!

"Faith, I—but—well—" I stammered.

Faith pressed her finger to her lips. Oops! No talking out loud to Faith while others are around!

Patches jumped up, barked twice, and wagged his tail. I'm pretty sure Patches can see Faith too.

Faith did a triple flip through the air and landed on my shoulder. "Mr. Boxer will come around if you and your friends find the right way to present your idea to him," she whispered.

"I think Mr. Boxer was just taken by surprise when we cornered him at the roller rink with our idea," said Nicola. "We should talk to him again. Maybe next week sometime—at the hospital."

"Good thinking!" said Aunt Ella. "I can drive you there in the van."

Just then I noticed that Kirina had tears in her eyes.

"What's wrong, Kirina?" I asked.

Kirina looked up. I was relieved to see her smile. "I'm okay," she said. "I was just thinking about the kids at the hospital. When my little brother was there, I was so worried about him. But he got better. The nurses were real nice and all, but he did get lonely and bored. He said he wished he had more company. I know there are kids there right now who feel just like my brother did. And then I think how happy they'll be when we make them laugh with our puppet show."

Kirina's eyes filled with tears again. The rest of us got quiet with sadness and happiness all mixed up together.

"God is mighty proud of you girls," Aunt Ella finally said. "He is delighted when we share our love with others—especially with those who need a little kindness to brighten their day."

"Well, maybe God will help us convince Mr. Boxer that we're trying to do something good!" Becca exclaimed.

"When you need God's help with something, all you have to do is talk to Him, darlin'. That's what prayer is for," Aunt Ella said. (Mom calls Aunt Ella a *prayer warrior* because she talks to God all the time.)

"That won't be necessary!" a voice announced from the doorway. Jenny McBride had just arrived. "My daddy is on the board of directors at the hospital. I'll just have him tell Mr. Boxer to let us put on the puppet show for the children."

"Really, Jenny? Just like that?" Bailey asked.

"Of course! My daddy will do anything I ask him to do."

We all exchanged quick glances.

"There's a spot for you right over here, Miss Jenny," Aunt Ella said. "We've started on the puppets and backdrops—but you can catch up."

"I'm so sorry I'm late. We stopped by the roller rink to schedule a party for the Precious Girls Club. Won't that be fun?"

"How delightful!" Aunt Ella said, and she helped Jenny get settled.

As we worked on our puppets, I wondered if Jenny's dad really *could* convince Mr. Boxer. Maybe so. Mr. McBride *was* president of the Shine Community Bank, and he owned a lot of the businesses in town. And one thing was certainly true—Jenny's dad seemed to give Jenny whatever she wanted.

"Okay, girls," Aunt Ella said, "Mrs. Bennett is having her carpets cleaned next Friday, so we need someone to volunteer their home for our next meeting."

"We can meet at my house," Lidia offered.

"How lovely! Are you sure your grandmother and grandfather won't mind, dear?"

"No, ma'am. My grandma likes to make lots of things too. She said that anytime we wanted to meet at our house, it was okay with her."

"Well, you thank her for me, will you?"

"I will," Lidia said.

Lidia and Becca stayed to help clean up, and I noticed Lidia looking around on the floor.

"Did you lose something, Lidia?"

"Yes. A button from my suspenders popped off again. It's the third one I've lost this month. Oh, well. It's no big deal. See you guys on Monday!" she called, skipping down the steps with a wave.

Becca and I waved back.

"Why does she always wear those overalls?" Becca asked.

"Beats me," I shrugged.

"Jenny teases her about them—and her messy hair."

"Jenny teases *everybody!* Do you think she'll really get her dad to talk to Mr. Boxer?"

"Probably. Not many people say no to Jenny," Becca laughed.

I smiled back, but I couldn't quite laugh—in case Faith was listening.

CHAPTER TWO

Second Chances

I went to my room. I had a math test on Monday to study for, and if there was one subject that gave me trouble, it was math. I really liked my teacher, Miss Marla, but her way of figuring problems was much different from the way I had learned at my old school.

"This is so firstrating!" I grumbled.

"You mean *frustrating.*"

Faith peeked around the corner of the desk.

"I certainly do mean it!" I pouted. "I don't like math one bit."

"The way you were talking today, I'd say you don't like your friend Jenny, either." Faith flew over and sat on the edge of my math book. "Sounded to me like she was making an effort with setting up the roller skating party and all . . ."

I rolled my eyes. "She's not making an effort, Faith. She's just trying to show off. Besides, she hasn't been all that nice to me since I moved here, you know."

"She's been nicer ever since she joined the Precious Girls Club—don't ya think?"

"Well, yes . . ." I admitted. "But she still acts stuck-up sometimes. And she's rude when she wants her own way."

"Guess she has some learning to do. But God loves Jenny, and He expects you to love her, too—and forgive her. If you just keep showing her your friendship and kindness, she'll come around. After all, everybody messes up."

"Some more than others," I said under my breath.

Faith tapped her finger on my book.

I sighed a big sigh. Sometimes it's hard to listen to someone who is right all the time. But Faith *is* my best friend. In fact, I don't know how I'd have gotten through the move to Shine if it hadn't been for Faith. My heart was so sad about moving away from my friends. Daddy seemed to know how I felt. He bought my sister Anna and me the most beautiful snow globes to cheer us up. Inside were lovely angels that danced in the swirling snow—I just loved mine. Imagine my surprise one day when I was alone in my room and my snow globe angel actually flew out and floated over my head! Well, that was my introduction to my very own guardian angel, Faith. Pretty super, don't you think?

Faith tapped her fingers again. "God gives people second chances—so, why shouldn't you?"

"Okay," I scowled. "I can give her a second chance. But, do I need to give her a third?—and a fourth?"

"Hmm . . . How many times should we forgive someone . . .? What does God say about that?" Faith fluttered over to my Sunday-school Bible and flipped through the pages. I looked down to where she was tapping her toes on a page.

"Seventy times seven?" I said. "Are you kidding me? I'm not real good at math, but I sure do know that's a *lot*!"

"It's actually four hundred—"

"What?"

"—and ninety."

"Four hundred ninety? Four hundred ninety chances? But—but—that would mean I'd be forgiving her my *whole life*!" I exclaimed.

Faith flew over and kissed the tippy-top of my head. "See, there. You *are* good at math."

I just groaned, got up, and went over to my closet. I pulled out a pink sweater and held it up as I looked in the mirror. Faith took off like a rocket and spun around me several times before landing on my shoulder.

"I like that color on you," she said.

"Yeah, but it's old," I grumbled as Faith flitted about, did a somersault, and landed on my right shoulder. "Don't you ever get dizzy?"

"Sometimes!" she yelled, toppling over backward.

I shrieked and twirled around to catch her, but she was already flying over my bed, giggling.

"You scared me!"

"Who scared you?" Anna asked. My sister had come into my room and was standing in the doorway. "Wait! Don't even say it. You were having a conversation with Miss Angel Wings, weren't you?"

I nodded. (Anna's snow globe angel did not fly around her room and talk to *her*—obviously.)

Anna looked in my room and shook her head. "Dinner will be ready in ten minutes. Mom said don't be late." She spun on her heel and disappeared into the hall.

"Her name is Faith," I called out.

I don't know if she heard me or not. I looked back at Faith and the two of us giggled.

CHAPTER THREE

I Scream for Ice Cream!

"Katie, you've hardly touched your dinner."

"I'm not hungry, Daddy. Would you like my pork chop?"

"Your father would like for you to eat it," Mom answered. "You've been so quiet since you got home from school, honey. What's up?"

"Jenny McBride promised that her dad would get Mr. Boxer to let us have the puppet show for the kids at the hospital. But Mr. McBride didn't talk to him—he said that Mr. Boxer knew how to run the hospital."

"Jenny McBride didn't get her way?" Anna asked. "Call the newspapers!"

"This is one time I wish she would've gotten her way," I said. "Now we still have to come up with a way to convince Mr. Boxer."

"Maybe you caught him on a bad day at the roller rink," Daddy said. "Don't get too worked up till you've at least given him another chance."

"That's true. It was just last month that Miss Marla gave you a second chance on that math test you did poorly on," Mom reminded me.

Math. Yuck.

"And last week you received *several* chances to get your chores done," Daddy winked.

"Do you figure we're going to have to give Mr. Boxer four hundred and ninety chances, Daddy?"

"If that's what it takes, kiddo!" Daddy laughed. "You're paying attention in church."

"Something like that," I grinned, hoping that Faith was listening. "I just hope Mr. Boxer will give us another chance too."

"I'm sure he will," Daddy assured me. "Now, try and eat a little more dinner, young lady."

"Okay, Daddy. If I eat my dinner, can we have ice cream later?"

"Yes," said Mom. "I just bought a gallon of chocolate marshmallow."

"Oh," replied Katie, "I meant, can we go to the ice cream parlor that just opened downtown."

"Gee, honey, I don't know," said Mom. "We have ice cream here—and it's not really in the budget this week."

"But everybody is talking about how many flavors they have and how yummy it is! Please?"

"We went out to a movie the other night," Daddy reminded me. "There will be plenty of time to visit the new ice cream parlor."

"But, Daddy . . ." I pleaded.

"Another time, Katie," said Daddy firmly.

I scowled and picked at my food. "Some of the girls have been there a whole bunch of times. I just wanted to go this once," I mumbled.

After Anna and I finished doing the dishes, I went upstairs to lay out clothes for the next day.

"Wear this," Faith said, flying over to a bright-green shirt with a white collar.

"I wore that on Tuesday," I told her. "I really need some new clothes."

"I know a wonderful way to make something old seem brand-new!"

"Really? Do you know magic?" I asked.

"No, silly. All you have to do is find something different to wear with it—like a pair of shoes, a piece of jewelry, or even a scarf."

"I don't have many shoes. I don't own a scarf, and I only have two necklaces," I complained.

"Munchkin, you've got very nice clothes. I really don't think you have to worry," Faith said.

"Not according to Jenny McBride. She said I look 'drab.' "

"Is that what this is all about?" Faith asked as she hovered right in front of me.

I shrugged my shoulders.

"You're not going to let Jenny McBride do your thinking for you, are you?"

"No," I insisted.

"Oh? Who was talking about the new ice cream parlor after school today?" Faith asked.

"Jenny," I admitted.

"And who are you trying to impress with what you wear?"

"No one!" I pouted.

Faith put her hands on her hips and cleared her throat—loudly.

"Okay," I said, "maybe I *do* care what she thinks. But so does everyone else. If *she* thinks I look drab, then other kids must think so too."

Faith flew over to my dresser, picked something up, and flew back over to me. "Hold out your hand," she ordered.

Faith slipped a pretty charm bracelet onto my

wrist. It was the special bracelet Mom and Aunt Ella had made for me to remind me of the many ways I was precious to God. The charms made sweet tinkling sounds.

"Some things are more important than the way you look. God made you to be a good friend," she said, holding up each charm. "He made you to be creative, caring, and funny. And God made you to be a good helper too. All of these virtues make you precious just the way you are, Katie. All you have to do is be yourself."

I looked at my beautiful bracelet. Maybe Faith was right. I gave her a big hug. She was my best friend in the whole world and always seemed to know how to cheer me up.

CHAPTER FOUR

A Bumbling Talk

Jenny led the way through the automatic glass doors of Shine Community Hospital. Aunt Ella had agreed to drive us over to talk to Mr. Boxer. We walked down the white hallway, got into the elevator, and headed up to Mr. Boxer's office.

In the elevator Jenny had been fidgety, but she seemed okay once we got out into the hall.

"Ewww!" she said. "Did you see that man on the elevator with the bandages?"

"Yes. So?" said Nicola.

"It was just creepy," said Jenny. "I don't like being around sick people."

"Then, why did you want to come with us to the hospital?" Bailey asked.

"Because I'm very good at talking to grown-ups," Jenny bragged. "I'll be able to explain our plan to Mr. Boxer."

Aunt Ella smiled. "Well, I'll hang back and let

you girls do the talking," she said. "But if you need any help . . ."

"Thanks, Aunt Ella," I whispered.

In the office area, people were answering phones, working on computers, and rushing around with file folders.

An older woman with pretty hair was sitting in front of Mr. Boxer's office, typing at her computer. She turned toward us and said, "How can I help you today?"

"We would like to see the president of the hospital, please," Jenny said with confidence.

The woman smiled. "Mr. Boxer is busy right now. Perhaps I can help you."

"Perhaps, but I don't think so," Jenny responded.

The woman looked amused. "I see," she said. "And why is it you need to see Mr. Boxer?"

"We came to offer the hospital a wonderful opportunity, ma'am," Jenny explained. "It will only take a minute of his time."

"Ah! Well, as I said—"

The door of Mr. Boxer's office opened and he came bustling out with his arms full of folders. "Delores, here's everything you'll need for—" He stopped when he saw us. "My, my, what a lovely group of young ladies," he said. I don't think he recognized us from the roller rink.

Delores stood up and took the files before they slipped from Mr. Boxer's arms. "These girls have a wonderful opportunity to discuss with you, sir," she said in a businesslike voice.

"Oh . . . er, I . . ."

"It will only take a minute of your time."

Thank you, Miss Delores! I thought.

Delores winked and waved us into the big office. Mr. Boxer nervously peered at us over his glasses as he sat down behind his cluttered desk.

Jenny launched right in. "We would like to present a puppet show in the lounge for the sick children during Shine Festival week."

"Oh, ah-huh, I see," said Mr. Boxer, fumbling

with a paper on his desk. "Thank you for offering, but, I—well, I—surely you girls can find somewhere else to do your puppet show."

"But, sir, the hospital is—" started Lidia.

Jenny placed a hand in the air to silence her.

"We're from the Precious Girls Club, and we chose to help the Shine Community Hospital as part of our next outreach project."

"Commendable, commendable, but, well," Mr. Boxer bumbled, "if you really want to help, perhaps you might consider a fundraiser. Perhaps . . . a Walk for Wellness. That's very popular with the young people."

"We put a great deal of thought into how we can help, sir," Jenny continued. "And the group decided on a puppet show. If you will just give us your permission, we'll be on our way."

Be on our way? Jenny sounded so grown-up!

There was a long pause. Mr. Boxer stood up and smiled. We breathed sighs of relief.

"I'm sure you've done a fine job with your puppet show," he began. "But there must be plenty of places more suitable for a show. Why, during the festival you could set up your stage right downtown."

We started to protest.

"I'm sorry, girls. Thank you for dropping by," he said with a wave. "Delores will give you some lollipops."

We thanked Delores, but did not wait for lollipops. We trudged toward the elevator, where some other people were waiting. One person was in a wheelchair.

"Hold on!" Jenny said. "Let's go back and get lollipops. We can take the next elevator down."

"I'm not going back for a silly lollipop," Nicola said. "Let's just get out of here."

"No, I don't want to go down right now."

"C'mon, Jenny. Let's go home," Kirina said, giving her a tug.

But Jenny wouldn't go. "I'll just walk down the stairs," she said.

"Six flights?" I asked.

"It's good exercise," she called, heading toward the stairwell.

Gee, I thought, *Jenny sure does get upset about being around someone who's sick or hurt!*

CHAPTER FIVE

A Humbling Talk

"Faith, please leave me alone," I said, not in the mood to talk.

She was trying her best to cheer me up, but it wasn't working. Jenny had made fun of my kitty sweatshirt in front of the entire class that day. To top it off, our puppet show was rejected—again!

Faith zipped by, looped around the room and landed on my dresser. "What's wrong, Munchkin?"

"Jenny McBride showed up in school today with a new outfit, and I can't remember the last time I got something new."

"Gee, how do you think I feel?" she asked. "I have to twirl about with the same dress and the same pair of wings every day."

I looked at my beautiful guardian angel. "You're the prettiest angel I've ever seen, Faith. I wish I could be as pretty as you. If Mom would just get me some new clothes—"

"Oh, Katie, you don't need new clothes to look pretty—you look good in anything."

A smile sneaked over my face.

"That's better! Your smile is much prettier than your pout. Say, I've got a new joke for you. Would you like to hear it?"

•   •   •

"Well, kiddo, I'm sorry your talk with Mr. Boxer went so poorly," Daddy said after dinner.

Mom was cutting up brownies—yum!

"We tried so hard," I said. "Maybe Mr. Boxer doesn't like puppets."

"Well, don't give up. You girls will think of something."

"Do you think so, Daddy?"

"I wouldn't joke with you."

"Oh, that reminds me," I said. "Faith told me a funny joke today."

"Can I eat my brownie up in my room?" Anna asked, rolling her eyes.

"Just don't drop any crumbs," Daddy called after her. "So, what's the joke?"

"What weighs five thousand pounds and wears glass slippers?"

"Hmmm . . . we give up," said Daddy.

"Cinderelephant!"

Mom and Daddy laughed and I beamed. I just loved making people laugh!

"You're quite a comedian," Daddy said.

"Yep! Maybe with Faith's help, I'll grow up to be a comet."

They laughed again—but I wondered why.

"You mean a *comic*," Daddy chuckled. "A comet is a big iceball flying through outer space."

"I don't want to be one of those. I think I'll grow up to be a comic, then."

"Just in case that doesn't work out, you better head upstairs and do your homework," Mom said. "And lay out your outfit for tomorrow."

"Oh! Speaking of outfits, Mom, I really need some new clothes."

Mom frowned. "Honey, we bought lots of new outfits when school started, and you have not outgrown them."

"But, my clothes are soooo not cool!"

"Cool, huh?" Mom's eyebrows went up. "Well, a balanced family budget is *very* cool—so I'd say we are the height of hipness, my dear. Now, head upstairs and finish your homework."

I grabbed Patches and ran upstairs as a tear slipped down my cheek. The minute I got to my room, Faith swooped over.

"What's this?" she asked, wiping my tear.

"Didn't they like my joke?"

I frowned and turned away. "Mom won't take me shopping for new clothes," I pouted.

"Hmmm," she said. "It seems to me that God just wants us to be thankful for what we have, rather than be so worried about what we *don't* have."

Faith was not going to back me on this. "I *am* thankful for what I have—mostly," I protested, "but today is a hard day to be thankful. I spent the afternoon trying to convince Mr. Boxer to let us do something nice for him! What do you think of that?"

"When you put it that way, I wonder if your visit was about helping others or just getting your way."

I didn't know what she meant. I was trying to do something nice for the kids. I really was.

After I went to bed, I lay there thinking.

"Faith!" I whispered in the dark.

"What?"

"You really hurt my feelings tonight. I thought you were my guardian angel."

"I am."

"Then, aren't you supposed to guard me from getting hurt?"

"Yes, but that doesn't mean giving you anything you want. I love you, Munchkin. A guardian angel helps to guard you from big hurts, even if it means letting you feel little hurts along the way."

"I don't understand."

"You will someday, sweetie."

I sure did wish that day would get here soon.

CHAPTER SIX

Puppets and Pinches

Friday! I was anxious for the Precious Girls Club meeting at Lidia's house. Grandma Peters greeted us with a big smile. Lidia's grandpa had taken her sister and brothers to the park, so we had the whole house to ourselves!

Only . . . it was not a very big house. It was real cute on the outside—kind of like a cottage. We stepped into a snug little living room. And there on the floor was the most adorable kitten!

"That's Toppit Two," Lidia said. "When I was little, we got our first kitten. I used to giggle 'Top it! Top it!' when I wanted the kitten to stop tickling me with kisses. My family thought it was cute, so they called her Toppit."

"Where is she?" I asked.

"Oh, she's not here . . ." said Lidia. "When my ma and pa had their car accident, Toppit was in the car, too, so . . ."

We got quiet—but Lidia smiled, tugged at her suspenders, and said cheerfully:

"We were excited when Grandpa said we could get a kitten. We named her Toppit Two."

"I like the name," said Becca, picking her up. "Hey, what do you call a cat at the North Pole?"

"Beats me," Lidia answered.

"Santa Claws!"

That got us laughing.

Lidia showed us around her house. I was surprised by how tiny it was. Lidia and her sister shared a bunk bed in a room barely big enough for their bed and two dressers. Her brothers slept in the attic, which her grandpa had fixed up to look like a baseball park. There was artificial turf on the floor and four white "base" footstools. The top cushions lifted up to store toys. The walls were covered with baseball posters.

"My brother Bobby would love this room," Nicola said. "He's a big baseball fan—but he has so much junk, it would never fit."

There was only one bathroom, and the kitchen and living room sort of made one room. The curtains and blankets looked handmade. *This is like a storybook cottage*, I thought.

"Who wants a Peters-pop?" announced Lidia, serving a tray of homemade popsicles.

Yum! Lidia's grandma pushed the coffee table against the kitchen table, so some of us could sit on the floor as we ate "Peters-pops."

Aunt Ella arrived with our supplies, and she and Lidia's grandma hit it off right away. They both helped as we sorted out puppet materials.

Toppit Two jumped into my lap and rubbed her soft little head against my tummy. Her fur was super silky, and I liked the sound of her rumbly purr.

"Did you get red velvet, Aunt Ella?" I asked.

"It turns out it was quite expensive . . ."

"But I needed it for the king's royal robe!"

"So . . ." Aunt Ella continued, "I got this royal purple velveteen instead."

"But I thought you were going to—ouch!" A tiny pinch on my shoulder made me jump. Toppit hopped away to Bailey's lap.

"Are you okay?" Grandma Peters asked.

"Yes, ma'am," I said. "I think I just got bit by a mosquito or something."

Aunt Ella placed some bowls of buttons and sequins on each table.

"Any gold buttons?" I asked.

"Hmmm . . . I don't think so," said Aunt Ella, peering over her glasses as she sorted through the bowls. "I'm sorry, sweetheart."

"But, Aunt Ella," I pouted. "I really need a-yowwwch! That hurt!"

Faith popped in front of me, wagging a finger. I was about to protest, but she pressed her finger to her lips. She knew I couldn't say a thing without looking silly in front of my friends.

"I . . . umm . . . hit my funny bone on the table," I told everyone.

Faith giggled. I glared at her.

"Well, did you get the ribbon I needed?" I asked impatiently.

"Let me see," Aunt Ella said, scrounging around in her craft bag. "How about this? Isn't this lovely?"

"It's not rainbow-colored—noooooowwwch!" Faith had tweaked my ear!

"Oh, gracious!" Grandma Peters said.

"I stubbed my toe. I'll be fine."

Aunt Ella gave me a wink and pointed to some shiny red-and-blue ribbon.

Faith perched on my shoulder. "Last night you told me you didn't want everything your own way," she whispered.

"Here you go, Katie," Grandma Peters said. She came into the room with a baggie filled with all sorts of buttons. "I keep these on hand for Lidia's suspenders. She does tend to lose buttons."

"Wow, Grandma! I didn't know you had all those," Lidia smiled.

"I just picked them up at that wonderful second-hand store," she said. "I got you two more pairs of overalls while I was there."

Lidia's face lit up. "Thank you, Grandma!"

"You're welcome, love."

"You *like* wearing overalls?" Jenny asked.

"Oh, yes! They're my fave," she answered.

"She won't wear anything else," Grandma Peters laughed. "But her charm bracelet sure makes any outfit sparkle."

I beamed. The girls held up their wrists and smiled. Our Precious Girls Club charm bracelets really did make us feel special—and precious!

As we worked on our puppets, we practiced the jokes that the characters were going to tell during the show. We were cracking ourselves up—until Jenny blurted:

"Ooo, it makes me so mad that Mr. Boxer won't listen to us. I bet he wouldn't even laugh at these jokes. He's just a—"

"—very busy man," broke in Nicola.

"He seems so nervous," added Bailey.

"It *is* a puzzle," said Aunt Ella quietly, sewing feathers onto a duck. "But he *is* the boss. I know your hearts are set on doing a show at the hospital, but . . ."

"Well, we can't give up," Avery said. "We just have to think of *how* we can convince him."

"I have always found," said Grandma Peters, attaching a trunk to an elephant, "that the 'how' takes care of itself when the 'why' is solved."

We all looked up.

"Huh?" Bailey asked.

Grandma Peters chuckled. "I just mean that, whenever I am faced with a problem and I am asking myself, 'How am I going to get this done?' then I simply begin to ask myself, '*Why* should I get this done?' If I have a strong enough reason, I somehow do manage to figure out *how* to do it. If I don't have a good enough reason . . . well, then"—she chuckled again—"I don't seem to get around to figuring out *how*!"

At that very moment, Toppit Two jumped right into the middle of a button bowl and started us giggling, "Top it, Toppit!" We went back to laughing, joke-telling, and puppet-making, without another word about Mr. Boxer. But I couldn't get him out of my mind, and I wasn't sure what Grandma Peters meant. *Grownups can be hard to figure out*, I thought.

When it was time to go home, we packed up our puppets and gave big thank-you hugs to Lidia and her grandma.

"Would you girls like a ride?" Aunt Ella offered as we loaded boxes into her van.

"We'll walk!" I said.

"And talk!" Kirina agreed.

A few steps down the sidewalk, Jenny said, "I had no idea that Lidia's house was so small. Did you notice there was only one TV?"

"Well, I liked her house," I said. "It was like a storybook house—real warm and cozy."

"But with hardly any closets," Jenny went on.

"Lidia doesn't need one—all she ever wears are overalls," said Avery.

"Well, we should do something about that."

"Like what, Jenny?" Bailey asked.

"We should all collect some clothes for her. In fact, her sister and brothers probably need some too. I don't think they have much—if you know what I mean."

"Yeah—Grandma Peters said she shops at the second-hand store," said Becca.

"But Lidia said she liked wearing those clothes," Nicola reminded us.

"What else would you expect her to say?" Jenny asked.

We shrugged.

"Lidia's backpack is a hand-me-down from her older sister. I saw the name scratched out," said Bailey.

"My brother would go crazy with so few toys," said Nicola.

"I'd go crazy without a TV in my room!" Jenny added.

"Won't she feel sorta weird if we bring over a bunch of clothes for her?" I asked.

"Let's do it secretly," Bailey suggested.

We all agreed. We'd gather clothes and some toys we didn't need and put them on their door-step on a day they weren't home.

"But, when? How?" asked Becca.

If we know the "why," we can figure out the "how," I thought.

"I know how," I said. "Tomorrow night is the Creative Arts Open House at school—Lidia's whole family is going early at 5:30 to help set up. Her big sister signed them up for that. We'll each collect our stuff, then meet at their house at 5:45 and leave the boxes on their porch."

It was a plan. I felt all glowy inside. It felt really good to plan something that would help someone else. And then it struck me—this had actually been Jenny's idea. Wow . . . she was kinda kind-hearted after all . . . maybe.

I waved goodbye to the others and headed home. I thought about Lidia. She seemed to have so little, and yet she never complained. I suddenly felt very thankful for everything I had, and was anxious to get home and tell my family.

CHAPTER SEVEN

Caring and Sharing

That night I went through my things and decided what to part with. I opened my closet and saw two long rows of clothes. Gee—everything looked too good to give away. And to think—I had been complaining about my wardrobe just a few days before. I felt bad for wanting so much stuff I didn't need.

"Hey! Don't feel too bad, Munchkin," Faith called out from across the room.

"But I do, Faith. I was being super greedy."

"But you learned something."

"Yes. Some things are more important than others. I don't really need more stuff. I'm just thankful for all the things that I already have."

Faith zipped around the room and did several triple flips, shouting, "Yippee! That's my girl!"

I laughed. "I'm thankful that God takes care of everything I need. He gave me a wonderful family, a nice house to live in, and good friends. God gave me special gifts and talents. Oh, yeah— God also gave me something else that's super special."

"What's that, Munchkin?"

"God gave me YOU!"

Faith circled around my head, shouting lots of "Hippy-Happy-Hurrays!" She zoomed over and landed on my pillow, a little out of breath. "Well, God gave me the special gift of being your guardian angel. And that's the best gift in the whole world."

We gave each other a big hug. Then I sorted through my things and decided what to share with Lidia. I chose two of my favorite sweaters, a new pair of sneakers, some pretty hair ribbons, and several CDs. I even decided to give Lidia a brand-new photo album that I'd saved up for with my own money. It would take me a while to save up for another one, but that didn't matter. Giving made me feel good on the inside.

When Mom and Daddy came in to say prayers and tuck me into bed, I told them what I was doing. They were really proud of me.

"Daddy, Lidia is so nice, and she never asks for anything. I don't even think she has anything that's new. When she saw my musical snow globe with Faith inside, she said she hoped someday she'd get one too. Could you get Lidia a snow globe angel? I think she might need a special angel to watch over her, just like Faith and Hope look out for me and Anna."

"That's one request I think I can manage," Daddy said.

"Oh, thank you, Daddy!"

I gave my parents a big squeeze and they kissed me goodnight. When they left the room, I whispered, "Faith! Are you sleeping yet?"

"Not yet."

"What was that 'hows' and 'whys' thing Grandma Peters was talking about? How will that help us with Mr. Boxer?"

"House and wise thing?" asked Faith. "Not sure about the house thing—but the wise thing may mean looking into your heart and asking God for wisdom and guidance."

I smiled and folded my hands. *Please, God, please help guide us. We want to do a puppet show for the kids at the hospital. I know You can show us the way.*

For the first time all week, I fell right to sleep. When I woke up the next morning, I was ready for a brand-new day!

CHAPTER EIGHT

The Whys Have It

Saturday! The Precious Girls Club met early at Camp SonShine, where Daddy works as the director. We used his workroom and he helped us build the big puppet stage. After measuring, cutting, hammering, and stapling, all that was left to do was to paint it.

"Great job!" Daddy said, as Patches barked an approval too. "I have some work to do down at the dock. You girls can paint, and I'll be back to help you pack. Be sure to clean up," he added.

Painting was fun. We used a bright red and a forest green, and Bailey added yellow polka-dots and pink stripes in a really cool design. We stood back to observe our work.

"Mrs. Wilson would be so proud!" said Kirina. "I don't do too well in her art class, but, hey—this looks great!"

"We couldn't have put it together without all your good measuring, Kirina," said Becca.

"Yeah," I added. "I wish I were good in math, like you. Hey, I know something I'm good at!"

I disappeared for a minute, then returned with ice-cream bars from the freezer. "Daddy said I could treat you all. They're on the house—or, camp!" I laughed.

We kicked back and enjoyed our snack. We didn't even mind when it was clean-up time. We pulled out the mops and sponges and set to work with a bucket of sudsy water.

Slosh—wipe—luckily the paint was easy to clean off the wooden floor. I started whistling, and a couple of the girls joined in.

Faith suddenly zipped in front of me and sang out, "Superrific! The Lord loves a cheerful worker."

Patches barked excitedly and leaped at Faith. He bumped into me, and my sponge landed right on top of Jenny's head.

Just then, Faith swooped away from Patches and flew at my head. I stepped back—*splat!*—right into a bowl of red paint and fell into Bailey.

"Hey!" Bailey tumbled into Kirina.

"My hair's all wet," said Jenny. She grabbed a paintbrush, plunged it into the soapy water—then wiped it all down my back.

"Red paint—on my shoes!" wailed Becca.

Patches was still leaping at Faith as Faith darted in and around us. I tried to grab him, but I slipped on some water and this time landed in the yellow paint—splashing it everywhere.

"Yellow paint—on my shirt!" cried Avery.

My back was sopping wet, I was sitting in yellow paint, and Jenny was *laughing* at me. I grabbed a brush, dipped it into green paint, and flicked it at her. *Splat*—right on her cheek. She stopped laughing, but the rest of us cracked up.

Don't leave me out!" said Lidia, taking a sponge and dousing her own head with water.

Nicola was standing back with her arms crossed, looking so much older than us.

"Aw, come on, Nicola," said Kirina, flicking pink paint onto her hair, "join the club!"

Well, that did it. Our "clean-up" turned into a wet and messy paint war. Colors flew, water splashed,

Patches was bounding after Faith, and soapsuds were everywhere. I guess Daddy heard us squealing with laughter, because we suddenly looked up and—

"Well," said Daddy, looming over us.

Oh, no! I thought.

"Mr. Bennett," stammered Nicola, "we—"

"It all started—" blurted Kirina.

Daddy laughed. "It's okay," he said. "You girls are having fun—and that's all part of the Precious Girls Club, right? Sometimes you just have to get silly and laugh—and be kids."

I beamed, as paint dripped down my face.

"You mean, you're not upset about the mess we made?" asked Bailey quietly.

"Nope," said Daddy. "It'll clean up with soap and water. I'm just so impressed with your stage. Wow! The kids will be excited when they come down to the hospital lounge and see that!"

"If we even get to *do* our show," grumbled Jenny. "Mr. Boxer hasn't given us permission. And we can't figure out *how* to convince him."

"Really?" said Daddy. "If your show is half as funny as you girls *look*, it should be a huge hit. And after all, laughter *is* the best medicine."

"Yeah, well, Mr. Boxer doesn't seem to care about our show."

"But I know he cares about the kids in the hospital," added Daddy.

I felt a tiny tug at my earlobe, and Faith's voice whispered, "Time to wise up, Katie. You asked God for guidance. Have you figured out the 'why'?"

My face must have looked funny, all scrunched up in thought. Everyone was staring at me. Then, like a light coming into my head, it hit me.

"You guys," I said, "Mr. Boxer doesn't know our puppet show is so funny. Laughter *is* like medicine—and laughter would be great for the kids in the hospital—right? Maybe we've been wanting to do the show because it would make *us* feel good inside. But that's not a good enough reason. You know why we've just *got* to do this? Because we want to help the kids feel better—and we have the right medicine for that—laughter!"

"Yeah, that's right," said Becca. "How could Mr. Boxer say no to that?"

"I think you should go right over there and ask him," said Daddy. "He goes home about noon on Saturdays. If you hurry and clean up, I bet we can get there before he heads out."

Wow, did we clean that place fast! Mops, sponges, and sudsy water were once again flying. After Daddy's thumbs-up, we piled into his van and drove to Shine Community Hospital.

We found Mr. Boxer right outside his door. When he saw us walk up, he looked a little nervous and turned to duck into his office.

"Mr. Boxer!" said Nicola. "We've come to talk to you about the puppet show for the kids. It's so funny—and you should see the stage. It will be awesome in the lounge!"

"Oh, dear, I am sorry, girls, but we just can't—" Mr. Boxer stopped and studied us. "Well, well. I'd say your stage is green, red . . . let's see . . . yellow . . ."

We looked at each other. We had cleaned up the floor, but our hair, faces and clothes still had splats of paint. Bailey giggled.

I stepped forward.

"Mr. Boxer, what we have is not just a show. It's medicine! It really is! We do jokes—and it's hilarious! The kids will laugh like crazy. Trust us. We know. We're kids!"

A smile lit up Mr. Boxer's face and his eyes looked very kind. "That's the best reason of all to do this show," he said.

We started to cheer, but Mr. Boxer put up his hand. "Let me explain why I cannot permit the show. We simply cannot bring all the children to the lounge. Many of them should not be moved from their rooms. Some are connected to equipment that is helping them get better. I care about each and every one of these children. How can I tell some that we have a special show for them, but not for the others?—the very ones who would enjoy it the most?"

Silence.

How could this be? I thought. *Didn't we have the right "why"?*

I looked at the other girls. Jenny was kind of pale. "Hey, are you okay?" I asked.

Jenny nodded, but she didn't look at all like her "normal" self. She faced Mr. Boxer and quietly said:

"Mr. Boxer, sir—what if we did the show in each child's room? May we do that, please?"

Kirina and Becca exchanged glances. Nicola said, "But, Jenny—you get so nervous if you're close to sick people."

"I'll do it," Jenny proclaimed. (The old Jenny was back!) "I can do anything I want to. And I want to hear the kids laugh!"

"Sold!" said Mr. Boxer.

"Sold?" we said, confused.

Mr. Boxer laughed. "That means, yes! If you can do the show for each child, I will permit it. It's going to take you all day though, you know."

"Oh, that's okay, sir." "Cool" "Alright!" "We did it!" Thanks, Mr. Boxer." "Yes!" "No problem!" "Thank you, thank you!"

"You certainly are a determined group. And, I must say, I am touched by how kindhearted you are. What did you say your group was called?"

"The Precious Girls Club!" we chorused.

"My, my. You *are* precious, indeed. I'll have Delores put together a schedule for you during the week of the Shine Festival."

It wasn't until Daddy was dropping off Lidia at her home that Avery suddenly said, "Hey! Our big stage will probably barely fit in a hospital room. How are we going to lug that thing up and down the halls?"

"Got it covered," announced Kirina. "Look!"

Kirina had drawn plans on notepaper for a small stage. "I've designed it to come apart easily so we can set it up in each room. We can make it and paint it at our next club meeting. No problem."

"How'd ya figure all that out?" I asked.

"Oh, simple. It's just math."

Math simple? Ha! I thought.

CHAPTER NINE

Boxes of Blessings

Right after dropping off Lidia, we firmed up our plans to meet at the Peters' house with the clothes and toys we had collected.

"5:45, right?" asked Avery.

"Yep," said Jenny. "This'll be so cool!"

And it was! At 5:45, we each showed up with a small box. When all seven boxes were placed on the porch, it looked like a lot.

At the Arts and Crafts Open House, it was fun showing our art projects to our families but the real fun was exchanging glances and giggles.

That night, after I told Faith about my all-time-best-day-ever-ever-ever, I prayed:

Dear God, thank you for the joy I feel. Thank you for your guidance, and showing us how great it is to share kindness with others. It makes me feel so good inside that sometimes I think I'll just burst! Amen.

On Monday I couldn't wait to get to school. Maybe Lidia would be wearing one of my favorite sweaters! What would she say about all her new things?

I was getting my homework out of my folder when I saw her come into the room. Huh? She was wearing the same old overalls she always wore. I looked over at Becca. She shrugged and looked just as puzzled as I felt.

During lunchtime we tried to make conversation, but it was hard. We kept waiting for Lidia to mention the boxes of goodies.

During recess, Lidia didn't say a peep about any new clothes or toys.

The day ended without one word—not one word—about our surprise boxes.

Tuesday came—and still nothing! Lidia had on overalls as usual. Same on Wednesday. Then Thursday. By the time Friday rolled around, we were really bummed that our boxes had not been a big hit at the Peters' house.

"Don't be too upset, Munchkin," Faith said as I walked home from school Friday. "You did your part—and it felt right—right?"

"Yes," I admitted.

"God decides how best to use our gifts. You did your part. Let God do His."

The Precious Girls Club gathered in our garage that afternoon to put together the new stage. It didn't take us more than an hour because Kirina's dad had already cut the boards and drilled some holes in them. We just hammered in pegs, and Kirina showed us how easy it was to set up and take apart. Then we painted it—and this time, I made sure Patches was inside the house!

As we were cleaning up, Mom came into the garage, carrying a bunch of Hawaiian leis.

"I've got a surprise for you in the back yard," she announced. "Who wants to dance the hula?"

We cheered and ran to the back yard. Wow, a Hawaiian luau! Tikki torches were lit and

cardboard palm trees lined the patio. Mom gave us each a colorful lei and a grass skirt. Tropical music was playing and we wiggled around trying to do the hula dance. Then we did the limbo! We looked silly, but it was fun.

Aunt Ella came out with ham-and-pineapple kabobs and a big platter of veggies and dip. Yum! But the best treats were the melon-and-banana smoothies with little umbrellas in them.

"We're celebrating how precious you all are," Aunt Ella said. "Each one of you has worked very hard to make puppets and a stage—"

"Two stages!" declared Nicola.

"Two stages!" laughed Aunt Ella. "And you've done it out of kindness for others. We're so proud of you. You have many talents and gifts, and it's wonderful to see you share them."

"Speaking of sharing," said Lidia, "I've got a really cool story to tell."

We tried not to gasp. Was this it? Was she going to tell about the surprise boxes?

"Last Saturday, when my family came home from the open house at school, we found a ton of stuff on our porch."

"Really?" Becca asked with a big smile.

"Seriously! We have no idea who left it. There were nice clothes, shoes, a bunch of toys, and even some CDs. We couldn't believe it!"

"That's amazing," Avery said. "So, why aren't you wearing any of the clothes?"

"Oh, it wasn't for us," Lidia explained. "Grandma helps out at the church a lot, so someone really nice must have left the boxes for her to drop off at the church."

"You didn't need any of it?" Jenny asked.

"Nah. We don't have a huge house or lots of fancy clothes and toys, but we have lots of love and more than we need. Oh, you guys, it was *such* a blast taking the boxes to church the next day to donate—you just *can't* imagine!"

"Oh, I think they can," Aunt Ella said, winking at us as we sat there with stunned faces and warm hearts.

We did our part. God did His.

CHAPTER TEN

Curtain Up!

"Why didn't the Dalmatian like to play hide and seek?" asked the fireman puppet.

"He was always spotted!" said the dog.

Jimmy sat up in his hospital bed and laughed. That made the rest of us laugh too. Avery elbowed Becca behind the stage to get her to say her next line. Becca muffled a giggle.

"Where does a monkey go when he loses his tail?" asked the snake.

"The re-tail store!" laughed the monkey.

This time it was Avery who could barely say her line. "A baby snake asked his mommy, [uncontrollable giggling] 'Are we poisonousss?' [more giggling] 'Why do you ask, sssweetheart?' his mom said. [outright laughing] 'I jusssst bit my tongue!' "

Jimmy cracked up the whole time, and his mom had happy-tears when she hugged us.

After that first performance, we couldn't wait to do more. Our stage was a snap to set up, and Delores went with us from room to room, telling us about each child. The last room was dimly lit.

"Suzy was burned," whispered Delores, "and her head is bandaged. She's been in a lot of pain, so don't be discouraged if she doesn't laugh much."

At first, Suzy didn't respond to our elephant jokes. But when Joe King came out (that was *me*, by the way!) and said, in a *very* silly English accent, "Do you know *why* I go to the dentist, young lady? To get my teeth *crowned*! And do you know what color my royal burps are? Royal *burple*!"—Suzy suddenly burst into peals of laughter! And she giggled the rest of the show.

Mr. Boxer met us outside Suzy's door.

"Girls," he said, "this was the best medicine these children could have. The doctors, nurses, and I can't thank you enough for your kindness. Please come back—anytime! Oh, and one more thing . . . Why did the kitty go to the hospital?"

We snickered. "Why?"

"To get a CAT scan," he chuckled.

We were the happiest group of girls in the *whole world* that night, as we celebrated at the ice cream parlor—Aunt Ella's treat. Even Jenny was all smiles. "We need to do that again," she said. "We'd put doctors out of business!"

"I'm so proud of you," Aunt Ella said, "and I have a gift for each of you, to remind you that your *kindness* makes you precious in God's sight."

She handed out the sweetest butterfly charms for our bracelets. "Oh, thank you, Aunt Ella!" we cried with a super-big group hug.

Aunt Ella drove us home, saving Lidia for last. I reached for something in the front seat. "Before you go, Lidia," I said, "this is for you."

"What for?" Lidia asked, holding the pink box with the big bow.

"Just open it."

Lidia opened the lid. Inside was a lovely angel dancing among snowy white flakes. I lifted out the snow globe and turned the knob on the bottom. It began to play "That's What Friends Are For."

"Oh, listen!" Lidia cried. "It's beautiful! Is it really for me?"

"Yes. Her name is Joy. I know how much you liked mine and Anna's. I wanted to give you an angel to remember our friendship."

"I'll always cherish this, Katie. Thank you!"

A tear slid down her cheek as she hugged me.

Faith gave me a wink and blew me a kiss.

That night when Mom, Daddy, and Anna came to kiss me goodnight, there was something important I wanted to say to them.

"Okay, kiddo, shoot!" Daddy said.

"Thank you for loving me and forgiving me when I mess up. Thank you for helping me have faith in God and for having faith in me. I used to feel alone in this town. But now I feel a part of it."

We hugged and prayed together. Then Mom said a special poem—just like she always does before we go to sleep each night.

I loved you from the very start.
Your joyful spirit touched my heart.
You're sweet and kind—a spirit rare.
Your love, a gift you freely share.
And as you grow so gracefully,
I see all that you can be.
So be your best in all you do,
My precious daughter—yes, that's you!

Up next for the Precious Girls Club:
Book # 3

Project Precious Paws

"Weeeeeeeee!" I giggled, sliding across the glistening ice on Lake Lightning. It was a cold but beautiful day in Shine, Wisconsin, where we had moved last summer. I was heading to a Saturday meeting of the Precious Girls Club, a group my mom and aunt helped me start so I could meet new friends and use my talents to help others. Being in the club is the most fun I have ever had in my life!

"Whoaaaa!" I shouted as my feet slipped out from underneath me, and I landed on my bottom. "Yowch! That smarts."

The ice was super cold against my jeans, so I rolled over to stand up but saw the ice start to crack beneath me. I suddenly remembered Aunt

Ella's warning about walking on the ice unless the green flags were posted for ice-skating. I quickly glanced at the shoreline; the flags were red!

The crack got deeper, even without my moving. Water started seeping through, and within seconds, my mittens and knees were soaked. *Oh no!* I thought. *What am I going to do?* As I searched the shore for someone to help, the ice broke and my legs plunged into the icy water.

"Help!" I screamed, clawing at the shiny surface. No one was around!

"Hang in there, kiddo," came the sound of a comforting whisper in my ear. It was my guardian angel.

"Faith! What should I do? Help me!" I shrieked. "I'm so scared. I've never been this scared before—ever!"

"You will be okay, Katie. You must have faith, sweetie," she said, trying to keep me calm.

That was hard. I tried to kick my freezing legs

and pull myself up onto the ice, but the water was so cold it made them feel achy and heavy.

"Hang in there, Munchkin," Faith said again.

I am the only one who can see and hear Faith, so I knew she could not go and get someone.

Then I heard a noise behind me. Faith was right. I was so excited as I turned around to reach for whoever had come up to help.

"Ahhhhhhh! Nooo!" I screamed, slipping a little farther into the water. Hot tears streamed down my cold cheeks. A big dirty dog had wandered out onto the ice and I was afraid he was going to bite me or push me all the way in.

"Please! Somebody help!" I screamed again.

"Woof! Woof!" The dog's loud bark scared me and made me lose my grip on the ice.

"Ahhhh!" I yelled, losing my grip a bit more.

Read more in Project Precious Paws
in stores Summer 2009

Charms + Bracelet

Create your own personalized charm bracelet like mine with special charms that show what is precious about you!

Caring

Helpful

Faithful

Kind

Responsible

Loving

Snow Globe

This is just like the one my dad gave me — you can have your very own!

Huggable Plush

Here is a cuddly version of my pet pup, Patches.

For these and other products, visit preciousgirlsclub.com to shop online or to find a retailer near you.